MARIAN KEYES

NO DRESS REHEARSAL

Marian Keyes' first novel *Watermelon* was published in 1995, and she quickly became one of the best-selling Irish authors of all time. Her four novels, *Watermelon, Lucy Sullivan is Getting Married, Rachel's Holiday* and *Last Chance Saloon* have sold over 2.5 million copies worldwide. *Sushi for Beginners* is the title of her latest novel.
Marian lived in London for eleven years and moved back to Dublin three years ago, where she now lives with her husband.

NEW ISLAND

No Dress Rehearsal
First published November 2000
by New Island
2 Brookside
Dundrum Road
Dublin 14

1 3 5 4 2

A CIP catalogue record for this book is available from the British Library

ISBN 1 902602 32 3

The Arts Council
An Chomhairle Ealaíon

**New Island Books receives financial assistance from The Arts Council
(An Chomhairle Ealaíon), Dublin, Ireland.**

Typeset by New Island Books
Printed by Cox & Wyman, Reading, Berks.
Cover design by Artmark

The OPEN DOOR Series offers a unique experience in reading. In this second collection of books, with contributions from some of Ireland's best-loved authors, we bring you six short novels, ideal for improving your reading skills while at the same time enjoying all the benefits of a good story. There's something to suit everyone's taste here, with themes of love — lost, found and forbidden — to the challenges of growing up, the ups and downs of family life, and to what happens to people who are dead ... but don't realise it. And, like all good stories, we hope these books will open doors — of the imagination and of opportunity — for adult readers of all ages.

All royalties from the Irish sales of the Open Door series go to a charity of the author's choice. *No Dress Rehearsal* royalties go to Trust, a befriending, social and health service for people who are homeless.

ALSO IN THE SERIES

Joe's Wedding, Gareth O'Callaghan
The Comedian, Joseph O'Connor
Second Chance, Patricia Scanlan
Pipe Dreams, Anne Schulman
Old Money, New Money, Peter Sheridan

The Open Door series is developed with the assistance of the City of Dublin Vocational Education Committee and Bank of Ireland.

For Tony

Dear Reader,

On behalf of myself and the other contributing authors, I would like to welcome you to the second Open Door series. We hope that you enjoy the novels and that reading becomes a lasting pleasure in your life.

Warmest wishes,

Patricia Scanlan.

Patricia Scanlan
Series Editor

Chapter One

Lizzie has just died. She simply hasn't realised it yet.

You'd be amazed at how often this kind of thing happens. Usually to people who were never very popular in the first place. When everyone starts completely ignoring them, they just accept it. Like they'd always thought it might happen, anyway. Sooner or later.

This wasn't the case with Lizzie, though. She was a popular girl. She just happened to have a lot on her mind on the afternoon in question.

Anyway, what happened was, Lizzie was cycling home from work. Weaving her way through the cars. Most of the time, going faster than them. On the Ranelagh road she got caught by traffic lights. "Come on," she muttered. "Change!"

As soon as the light changed to green she took off like a hare out of a trap. She cycled out into the clear road, heading for home. Next thing, her bike slid on a patch of oil. In slow motion she saw herself flying straight into the path of an oncoming Volvo. She watched the wheels speed towards her. Far, far too close to her head. *This isn't happening*, she thought.

A film-reel of pictures raced behind her eyes. All of them about her. Aged four, falling out of a tree. The dog she'd had when she was seven. The coolest pair of cowboy boots she'd got when she was twelve. Her first romantic kiss. Her last day at school. Meeting Neil for the first time. Moving in with him. Going to work this morning. Leaving work this evening …

And then everything stopped. No more pictures. For a few shocked seconds she lay on the greasy road. Her cheek was pressed against the tarmac. So close that she could see hundreds of pieces of tar-coated gravel. They'd been smoothed by a million car tyres. So many little stones, she thought. Then, I wonder if I'm badly injured?

Slowly, carefully, she told her leg to move. It did so without sending hot agony shooting through her. This could only be good. She tried her other leg. No pain there, either.

Testing each limb, she gingerly climbed to her feet. All the while, she expected some body-part to object. But to her relief it looked like she had no bones broken. In fact, as she checked herself, it seemed that she wasn't even cut. How lucky was that!

It was then that she saw that the driver of the car had got out. He came towards her. His face was twisted into a mask of horror.

"It's okay," she said, shakily. "I seem to be in one piece. Luckily!"

To make him feel better she faked a laugh. But he paid her no attention. From the shapes he was making with his mouth, he seemed to be trying to talk. But he wasn't having much luck.

"I swear to God," she said, "I really am fine! Don't ask me how, but I am."

Still he didn't speak. Suddenly she went weak. She was hit by a longing to be at home.

She left the driver to his silent mouthing and got on her bike. By some miracle it was undented. And away she cycled. Leaving her still and bloody body lying beneath the car wheels.

As she wobbled off, she almost bumped into someone. A tall, pale figure in a long, black, hooded cape. He nodded at her in a friendly way. But she hardly noticed.

She still didn't know what had happened. Nor did she notice the crowd of curious and worried people gathering around her body. She didn't hear the ambulance siren in the distance. She didn't see the huge queue of cars along the Ranelagh Road. All delayed on their way home because her body was blocking the road.

But if she *had*, she would have burned with shame. Because she was wearing her worst knickers. They were arm-pit high and the colour of porridge. How could she not have realised that they'd get an audience? It was as good as *guaranteed*.

Most days Lizzie arrived home breathless and sweating, with her thigh muscles on fire. The cycling was yet another of her many efforts to get fit and skinny. Especially skinny. But today the journey felt oddly effortless. She seemed to sail along, as if the entire route was downhill.

Chapter Two

At the very moment that one of the ambulance men officially declared her dead, Lizzie arrived home. She shared a flat in Rathmines with her boyfriend, Neil. They'd lived there for a year-and-a-half. It was a bit of a kip. Which hadn't mattered so much in the first flush of love. But which had started to get on her nerves a bit lately.

She left her bicycle in the hall, and shoved her key in the lock. She took a couple of steps back, like she always did. Then she did a little run at her front door, heaving her shoulder against it. There was something wrong with the door. It kept sticking. And she kept meaning to do something about it. Like ring the landlord.

She could hear the telly. Neil was home. She looked into the front room where he was flung on the couch.

"That bloody door," she complained. She made her voice sound light and good-humoured because she was nervous. They'd had a row that morning — yet another one. In fact things had been going badly between them for quite a while.

What it came down to was this. They'd been going out with each other for two years. And living together for eighteen months. Lizzie wanted to settle down and Neil wasn't so keen. To put it mildly. (That was why she had other things on her mind when she was knocked down.)

She was thirty-two, and fed-up being a party girl. She wanted stability. To own their own place. To think about having children.

"That bloody door," she said again. But Neil didn't speak. He continued to stew on the couch like someone in a coma.

Lizzie swallowed and made herself ask, "So, how was your day?" She said it gaily, happily. Trying to pretend to him that she didn't really mind if he didn't make a commitment to her.

Of course she minded. She minded very much.

Lizzie wasn't the kind of woman who normally took nonsense from men. Shape up or ship out was her usual approach to romance. But the problem was that she loved Neil.

The smile died on her face as, still, he didn't answer. In fact he didn't even look up at her.

She hung around in the doorway, feeling frightened and foolish. She licked her dry lips and tried to think of another light-hearted remark. Nothing doing. All she could manage was to mutter, "I fell off my bike."

Still he ignored her. Not a word of sympathy.

So that's how bad things had become, she realised. Living under the same roof and not even speaking to each other. It hit her hard. All at once she found it difficult to breathe. She swung away from the living room and went to the kitchen. She rested her elbows on the worktop and gasped into her hands, fighting for breath. *Hot sweet tea* was the only thought she could latch on to. Hot sweet tea was good for shock.

She didn't know how good it was for the end of two-year relationships, however. Somehow she reckoned she'd need more than a cup of tea. More like a bottle of wine a night every night for six months.

As she searched around in the kitchen for something that resembled sugar — she *must* go to

Dunne's, she *must* get her life in order — the phone rang.

She cocked her ear at the front room. Then she heard Neil say, "What? I don't believe you. Oh, Jesus!" A few seconds later came the sound of the front door slamming shut (after first sticking slightly).

She ran out into the hall. What was going on? Where was he gone? She stared at the door, and thought about running after him. Then suddenly she felt too hopeless. What would be the point?

When she couldn't lay her hands on any sugar, she gave up on the idea of hot sweet tea. She just sat on the sofa, feeling very odd. She felt cold and dopey. Her ears buzzed and she couldn't seem to think properly. Maybe she was in shock after the accident, she decided.

Desperate for comfort, she wanted to talk to someone. So she rang her best friend, Sinead.

Sinead always made her feel better, even if she couldn't provide words of wisdom (and usually she couldn't). But at the very least Sinead had the decency to be almost more fed-up with her life than Lizzie. Like Lizzie, Sinead hated her job. But

Sinead's job was far more stressful than Lizzie's. Like Lizzie, Sinead had man-trouble. But Sinead's trouble was that she had no man at all.

But something was wrong with her friend's phone. Lizzie could hear Sinead perfectly but Sinead couldn't hear her. "Hello," she kept saying, "Who is it? Is somebody there?"

"Ah, shag it," Lizzie sighed. It wasn't her day. She hung up and rang again, but still Sinead couldn't hear her.

"IT'S ME," Lizzie yelled. "I fell off my BIKE and I'm MISERABLE and Neil has gone OUT without telling me where he's going —"

"Look, here," Sinead's voice threatened, "Are you the fella who wants to talk about my underwear? Because if you are, I've got something to say to you."

With that, a piercing whistle screeched down the line. If Lizzie had still had an eardrum it would probably have started to bleed. Rubbing her ringing ear, she hung up. She wouldn't be calling Sinead again this evening.

Poor Sinead, she thought. Obscene phonecalls were yet another cross that she had to bear.

So now who could she talk to? She could ring her mother, she supposed. Except she couldn't, because she'd only start giving out to her. Telling her it was her own fault she was down in the dumps. That she should never have moved in with Neil in the first place. "Why would he marry you when he's already getting what he wants from you?" she'd say.

No, she definitely wasn't ringing Mammy Whelan this evening. Nor was she going to ring her father. Not because he'd give out to her. Not at all! He'd barely say anything. All he ever said when she rang up was, "I'll get your mother". You stood a better chance of having a conversation with Shergar.

But she was mad keen to talk to someone. She'd have to ring the Samaritans at this rate. Or order a pizza just to hear a warm human voice.

But when she tried ringing the pizza delivery place, it turned out that it was her phone which was broken, not Sinead's. She could hear the pizza man, but he couldn't hear her. Which was funny because the phone had been fine earlier. It had obviously been working perfectly when Neil had got the call which had lifted him from the flat like a bat out of hell.

Now what, she wondered listlessly. She could always overeat, of course. Nothing like milling into a family-sized bag of crisps to keep the blues away. But there were no crisps in the flat. Worse still, she wasn't hungry. I *am* in shock, she realised. Bad shock.

The only time she ever skipped her evening meal was when she went for "just the one" after work. And ended up mouldy drunk on an empty stomach by half-eight. Too jarred to hold a knife and fork, and fit for nothing except bed.

"Cigarettes!" she thought, suddenly. "They'll do the trick. And so what if I've given them up."

Now, where had she hidden her emergency supply? She tried her tights drawer. Then the press in the bathroom. Then under her bed. But no joy. Just when she was losing hope, she remembered. She ran into the lounge and threw herself on a video case. *Please let this be the right one.* Quickly she pulled it open. And found ten Benson & Hedges inside.

"Aha!" She kissed the box two or three times. Then she lit a cigarette and pulled on it down to her toes.

But strangely, even that didn't make her feel better.

Chapter Three

Sinead finished blowing her whistle, then she slammed down the phone. The mystery knicker-discusser hadn't called in a while. She'd thought she'd got rid of him for good. Well, think again. Although he hadn't sounded himself. Maybe he wasn't well, she thought sarcastically. He hadn't done his usual heavy-breathing routine. Or attempted a discussion on the finer points of her underwear. All she'd really been able to hear was a type of faraway keening. A distant whistling. Almost ghostly.

Suddenly she felt slightly spooked. For no reason at all she flicked a glance around the room. Almost as if she was expecting to see something. She wasn't quite sure what. But *something*.

She prickled with unease, aware that she was alone in her flat. Uncomfortably aware. Then she jumped as the walls of her flat began to squeeze to the sounds of NWA booming from the flat above.

Alone? She wasn't alone. She was never alone as long as Wayne was living overhead.

Her jaw clenched tightly in familiar tension. She should move. Or complain to someone. Possibly even Wayne. But she was afraid of him. Him and his pit-bull.

The phone rang again. Quickly, she switched on her answering-machine. She wasn't in the humour to talk to the mystery knicker-discusser for a second time this evening.

The greeting played. *I'm not here right now, but please leave a message.*

"Sinead," a voice roared into the room. Sinead's heart sank. It wasn't the mystery knicker-discusser. She'd have preferred the mystery knicker-discusser. It was Ginger Moran, her boss.

"I know you're there," he bellowed into the room. "Where else would you be? Pick up the phone."

Sinead thought about ignoring him. But she knew what he was like. He wouldn't go away. So she gave in. She snatched up the phone and said curtly, "What?"

"What yourself," Ginger said cheerfully.

"What are you ringing me at nine o'clock for?"

"What are you ringing me at nine o'clock for?" he repeated in a namby-pamby voice.

She didn't speak. Then he snapped into action. "You never left me the bill of lading for the tobacco shipment."

"It's in your in-tray." She kept her voice even.

"*Where* in my in-tray?" Sinead had to stand by and listen to sounds of rustling, as Ginger pawed through sheets of paper. "Ah, I have it. See you tomorrow, don't be late. We've that delivery of ball-bearings coming."

"And thank you, too," Sinead said sarcastically, hanging up the phone.

Sinead had worked for Ginger Moran for a very long time. Too long, she often thought. She was twenty-four when she had taken the job. Just to fill a couple of months while she decided what she really wanted to do. And here she was, eight years later, still working for him.

He ran an import–export business. It operated out of a busy office and warehouse in Ringsend. And she suspected that a lot of his business deals were very slightly illegal.

He imported knocked-off cigarettes. Or stolen Nike runners. Or fake Hilfiger T-shirts. She reckoned he'd do anything if there was a couple of bob in it.

She didn't know why she stuck it. He was a mad-man. Demanding and narky. As well as her normal working duties, she had to do all kinds of other things for Ginger. Not just the usual stuff, like buying presents for his girlfriends. But organising dentist's appointments. Choosing new clothes for him. Keeping him up-to-date with *Coronation Street*. And if she missed the evening episodes, he insisted that she watch the weekend omnibus.

He treated her like a mix of wife and mother. And the worst thing about him was that he always knew when he'd pushed her too far. When that happened he'd suddenly become contrite and almost sweet. Telling her she was great. Giving her presents.

Mind you, they were only ever things like a box of stolen Nike runners. Men's ones. Miles too big. Or a carton of fake Marlboros. Not much use to a non-smoker like herself. She'd given them to Lizzie, who had lit one and then stubbed it out straight away. "Disgusting," she'd declared. "That's not tobacco. They must have used tea-leaves! Or worse."

In fairness, Ginger paid well. It was probably the one reason why she hadn't left before now. That and the threats, of course.

"If you ever leave me, I'll put a contract out on your life," he often warned her. This was meant to be a compliment. "If you ever hand in your notice, I'll kill you and then you'll be sorry."

Sinead half-believed him. There were enough dodgy characters in and out of the office. She was sure he'd be able to lay his hands on a hired killer if he needed one.

The phone rang once more, and Sinead tensed. Who was it this time?

"It's me again," Ginger bellowed. "Where's my stomach tablets?"

Seconds after she hung up, the phone rang *again*. God, it was all go this evening.

This time it was Shane, an ex-boyfriend. She hadn't heard from him in about six months.

"Come out for a drink, will you," he asked.

"Ah Shane, I'm knackered tired."

"How come? You're not still working for Ginger Moran, are you?"

"And what if I am?" Sinead said, huffily. When she'd been going out with Shane, he'd slagged her constantly about being Ginger's mammy.

"No wonder you're knackered," he laughed, "Being on-call twenty-four hours a day."

Well, she had to go for a drink after *that*. Just to show that she was able.

Chapter Four

Half an hour later she met Shane in the pub. He was a normal, nice-looking man. She was surprised by how good it was to see him. She was glad she'd made the effort to come out. She tried to remember why they'd broken up, and couldn't.

Sinead had a small stable of ex-boyfriends. For some strange reason she was still on speaking terms with them all. She didn't know how she'd managed that. Everyone else she knew spat when they mentioned an ex.

Maybe because none of her boyfriends had mattered that much to her. Oh, she'd liked them and all that. But not one of them had been The One.

Of course, she'd *thought* some of them were. When she'd first been going out with them. But it had always turned out to be a case of mistaken identity.

To be honest, Sinead wasn't even sure if she could be bothered hoping to meet The One any more. She was weary from the whole business. And look at the misery it brought to poor Lizzie, hanging around with that Neil. He was a decent enough man, she wasn't saying otherwise. But he was also thirty-three going on sixteen and very slow to make a commitment. She couldn't be doing with that.

Sinead was a romantic. But not really in the hearts and flowers way. More in the broader sense of the word. She dreamt about travel and adventure. Of freedom and excitement.

And she had no doubt in her mind that it would happen for her. At some stage. But at the moment her life was more about doing the immediate things. Buying her dad's birthday present. Washing her clothes. Hiding the grey that had the cheek to start appearing in her hair. These things *had* to be done. And when she was on top of everything, then she could start making her plans.

Of course, she didn't go round thinking this. Not out loud, anyway. But humming away at the back of her mind were thoughts of another life.

Once, a couple of years back, Sinead and Lizzie had gone to get their fortunes told. And the tarot reader had told Sinead that she'd find true love and happiness in a foreign country. Lizzie had got all excited about it. She urged Sinead to jack the job in and go off on an adventure. But Sinead clung to her demanding job and her awful flat with the noisy head-the-ball living upstairs. "You can't move countries just because some old biddy with a deck of cards says you should," she insisted.

"I know, but you *want* to go," Lizzie pleaded. "Why don't you go to have a look? Even if you decide you hate it, at least you'll have found out."

"It's low self-esteem," Sinead had laughed. "Because I'm *not* worth it!"

Chapter Five

At midnight Lizzie decided she'd better go to bed. But Neil still hadn't returned. In the cold, lonely bed, she lay staring into the darkness. There was no hope of getting any sleep. She was too worried. She had a horrible feeling that very bad things were about to happen.

Where was Neil? He'd never done this to her before. He was a decent fella. But where the hell was he? Was he with someone else? *In bed* with someone else?

No, she couldn't believe that. They'd had a row, that was all. Okay, so they'd had lots of rows lately. But he loved her. He'd told her he loved her. Only that very morning.

"I just don't want to get married," he'd said. "We're fine as we are."

"But ... but what would be the harm?"

"I love you," he'd said. "You're the woman for me. But I'm not ready for all that business. Buying a house. Having babies. Not yet."

"But you're thirty-three!"

"I still feel too young. Come on, Lizzie, we've a good life. We have a good laugh. Let's enjoy it!"

"But ..."

And then she'd said no more. Best not to push him too far.

But it looked like she might have pushed him too far. The alarm clock by her bed clicked as each second ticked by. Each tick sounded as loud as the crack of a whip. She decided she was getting a digital clock. At least they were silent.

She kept switching on the lamp to check the time. One o'clock. Half-past one. Ten past two. Each time, her panic got worse.

At five past three she heard a key in the lock, then a thump as a shoulder pushed the front door. Thank God! Thank God! He was home.

He barged into the bedroom, and turned on the light. His eyes were wild.

"Where were you?" she asked. Her voice shook.

But he just stared around the room, not really looking at anything. His eyes slid over her. As if he couldn't see her. Then, as she smelt the drink from him, she understood. He was jarred.

"Still not talking to me?" she asked. "Even though I'm worried out of my mind."

She watched his mad eyes fix on a pile of clothes on a chair. He picked a jumper off the top of the heap. It was one of hers. Then he sank onto the bed. As she watched in disbelief, he pressed his face into it. Was he going to puke? On her good jumper!?

But he didn't. Instead Neil took a deep breath and inhaled the smell of the wool. That threw her. She hadn't a clue what he was up to. But whatever it was, it was very odd. She eyed him, as he rocked back and forth, the jumper to his face.

After a while he got into bed, then turned off the light. Seconds later, in the darkness, she heard a noise from him. Again she thought he might be about to puke. Until she realised that he was … surely not? … *crying*?

The sound broke her heart.

"Let's be friends," she said softly. She couldn't be doing with this fighting. She moved across the sheets and pressed herself up against his back. But he shivered like a wet dog and drew away.

Badly hurt, she moved away again.

She thought she'd never be able to sleep as she was far too upset. But she did doze off. And when she woke up, he wasn't beside her. Terrified, she hopped out of bed and ran around the flat. There was no sign of him anywhere.

Of course, Lizzie wasn't to know that the night before, Neil had rushed over to her parents. To try to comfort them and himself. And that after he'd come to bed and nodded off, he'd only managed two hours sleep. At five a.m. he'd jerked awake. Wide awake, yet he still felt like he was in the middle of a horrible nightmare. When he went to the kitchen to boil the kettle, he found he couldn't bear being alone in the flat. Especially because he didn't *really* feel alone. Not after he'd found a fresh butt in the ashtray. Who had smoked that? Neil didn't smoke. Neither did Lizzie. Lately, anyway. So who'd smoked it?

Suddenly all his neck hairs were standing on end and he was pulling on clothes and racing back to her parents.

Lizzie knew none of this. All she could see was that he was gone again. Misery wrapped itself around her like a heavy, grey cloak. Things were much worse than she'd realised. He'd never behaved like this before.

Panic rose in her throat. She had to talk to him. This had to be sorted out once and for all. She decided to ring him at work as soon as she got in herself.

Half-heartedly she got ready for work. Then she did her daily ritual of standing on the weighing scales. This was to see if the cycling was having any effect. But instead of whizzing up to nearly ten stone, the needle on the scales didn't budge. Even when she bounced up and down, it stayed stuck at nought. Broken, she thought, like everything else in my life.

Chapter Six

Neil and Lizzie weren't the only ones who'd had a bad night's sleep.

Sinead had spent eighty-nine minutes between three and five a.m., worrying about all the work she had to do the next day. She got back to sleep but awoke exhausted.

By eight o'clock she was at work. The phone rang at ten past. Who could be ringing so early? Ginger probably. Telling her he couldn't remember how to breathe. Or asking her what side he parted his hair on. But it wasn't Ginger. It was Neil. What did he want?

"I've some bad news," he said.

Now what could that be? Had someone scraped the side of his car? Had Man U lost last night?

"It's Lizzie," he said. And immediately Sinead stopped her sarcastic thoughts. She felt a sudden and terrible fear.

"She was in an accident yesterday," Neil said.

"Where is she?" Sinead was already pawing for her bag. "Which hospital? I'll go now."

"No." Neil said. "You can't."

"Why not?"

"Because ... because she's ..."

Dead. What a funny word it was, Sinead thought, calmly. Dead, dead, dead, dead, dead, dead, dead. It was a good word for dead. Because it sounded so dead.

Neil was mumbling into her ear about removals, funerals. But she wasn't really listening. Her gaze was drawn to the floor beneath a filing cabinet. Look at how dusty it was. Thick with it. I suppose there wasn't enough space to get a brush beneath it. That'd be why it's so dusty, she thought.

"I'm at her parents," Neil said.

"I'm coming over."

As she was leaving, Ginger was just arriving.

"Where are you going?" he asked in alarm.

"Lizzie died," she said, trying out the new and strange words. Then she decided to try it another way to see if it felt any more real. "Lizzie is dead."

Ginger stared at her. "But where are you going?"

"To see her mammy and daddy. To help them and Neil with the arrangements."

"When will you be back? We've that big load of ball-bearings coming in today."

Carefully Sinead repeated, "Lizzie is dead. I don't know when I'll be back."

"Er, right. Make sure you have your mobile on." Then, too late, Ginger remembered his manners. "Sorry for your trouble," he muttered.

Chapter Seven

The morning was very misty as Lizzie cycled to work. She had to swerve more than once to avoid hitting people. They kept stepping out into her path, as if they couldn't see her. Puzzled, she put it down to the mist.

At the office she said a gloomy "Good Morning" to Harry the porter. But he point-blank ignored her. Her throat ached with the onset of tears.

Clearly something was in the air. Brenda, her secretary, had her head on her desk and was crying for Ireland.

Further down the hall Lizzie spotted her boss, Julie. Was she imagining things or did she look very sad and grim? In fact there seemed to be an air of misery around the place that wasn't quite the same as the *usual* air of misery. It had a different, deeper feel to it. Hey, Lizzie thought sarcastically, has somebody died?

When she pushed open the door of her little office, she stopped short. To her surprise, there were two people already there. They looked like social workers. The man had a beard and a brown hairy jumper. The woman had frizzy, purple hair and earrings that looked like she had made them herself. And probably out of milk-bottle tops, at that.

"Excuse me," began Lizzie, but the male social worker stopped her.

"Hello Lizzie," he said gently, "my name is Jim. Why don't you sit down, I'm afraid this may come as a bit of a shock."

"What's going on?"

"Please Lizzie, it's better if you sit down," said Jim.

Shakily she did so. "Is it Neil. Has something happened to him?"

"No, Lizzie, I'm afraid it's you."

"ME?"

"Yes, Lizzie." Milk-bottle-top woman spoke for the first time. "By the way, I'm Jan. Haven't you noticed anything … well … a little bit odd yesterday and today?"

"No," Lizzie said stoutly.

"Really?" Jan sounded like she didn't believe her.

"Alright, things have felt a bit strange, I suppose," Lizzie admitted, though she didn't want to. "But only because I was in shock from falling off my bike."

"Lizzie, I'm afraid that when you fell off your bike yesterday, you died," said Jim.

"Well I admit I was embarrassed," Lizzie said. "But anyone would be."

"No, I don't mean that you died of embarrassment," Jim said. "I mean that you died. That you are now dead."

Lizzie started laughing. "Ah, come *on*!"

"Lizzie, your reaction is quite normal."

Lizzie's patience snapped. This nonsense had gone on long enough. "What the hell are you talking about?" She raised her voice. "Who are you? Who let you in here!?"

"We are what you might call your welcome committee," Jan said. "Our job is to welcome you to your new plane. To sort out any little problems that you might have while you settle in. And nobody let us in here. We don't have to be let in, we can appear anywhere we like.

"Not that I'm showing off," she added hastily. "That's just the way it is."

"I don't know what drugs you're taking, I swear to God I don't." Lizzie had enough on her plate with a runaway boyfriend. She felt quite unable to deal with these two oddballs. Leaping up from her chair she ran to the door and called, "Brenda".

"No, don't do that," Jim said nervously. Oh dear, he had seen all this before and it still upset him. Even after all these centuries.

"Brenda!" Lizzie cried again. But Brenda — who was now typing with red eyes and sniffing and snorting like a rhino — seemed not to hear.

"BRENDA!" Lizzie shook her secretary's shoulder. She couldn't believe it when Brenda shivered like a jelly, but didn't react in any other way. She didn't even turn around. She simply continued typing.

Bloody hell! Lizzie had always known that Brenda wasn't too quick on any uptake, but it was almost like she had gone into a trance.

Right then! Time for the heavy guns! Angrily Lizzie marched down the hall to Julie's office. No better woman than Julie. She'd sort out these two trespassers, if anyone could. After a brief knock, she pushed the door open. Julie was having a discussion with Frank, another senior member of staff.

"I'm sorry to interrupt," Lizzie said, "but we've got a problem, Houston."

Lizzie's voice trailed off as she noticed several things all at once. Firstly, she noticed she was being completely ignored. Secondly, she saw that her diary was open on the desk. Julie was saying to Frank, "We'll cancel all the meetings she was due to have this week. Then we can brief Nick and let him take over ..."

"What are you doing with my diary?" Lizzie's voice was thin and high with outrage — and fear. "And why are you cancelling all my meetings. And giving my cases to Nick? I mean, what the hell is going on around here? Well?" she demanded.

Their heads remained bent over her diary. They didn't even look up.

"Well?" Lizzie demanded again, but she had started to shake.

"How did that door open?" Julie murmured, crossing the office. She stood before Lizzie, looked her right in the eye — and right through her. Then shut the door firmly in Lizzie's face.

For a few stunned seconds Lizzie stood, her nose almost touching the wood-veneer door. She'd been sacked. Hadn't she?

But a horrible suspicion was growing in her mind. Getting bigger and gathering force. Something was going on. And she had an idea that whatever it was, it was far worse than being sacked.

Panicking, she turned on her heel and ran down the hall, stopping at every office on the way. The same thing happened in each case. No one could see her and no one could hear her. When she laid her hands on people they shuddered and shivered.

Wheeling around in sweaty terror, she started back up the hall. The feelings of fear and nausea were starting to make sense.

Chapter Eight

She burst into her office, and found the two ghostly social workers still sitting there.

"I'm sorry you had to go through that," Jan said sadly.

"No one can see me," Lizzie screeched. She was no longer a successful insurance manager but more of a dead fishwife.

"That's because you're dead," Jan agreed.

"I'm not dead, don't be so stupid! How could I be dead? You pair of eejits, coming in here, talking crap ..."

Jim and Jan let her have her little rant. They were used to this sort of thing. All part of their day's work. It was as well to let her get her anger out of the way. Then they could talk calmly.

After a ten-minute tantrum, Lizzie paused and said sharply, "Why do you say I'm dead? Prove it to me."

Jim and Jan looked at each other, then Jim gave Jan the nod. You tell her.

"Didn't you notice Death the Grim Reaper standing by the accident yesterday?" Jan asked.

And once Lizzie thought about it, she *did* remember a tall, gloomy-looking man hanging around the accident scene.

"Well, yes," she admitted, "but I thought he was a student collecting for Rag Week."

"In July?" Jan asked with gentle humour.

"And no one could hear you on the phone last night," Jan reminded her.

"The phone is broken," Lizzie said quickly. Too quickly.

"It's not. It was working fine when your father rang Neil to tell him you'd died. And that business with the weighing scales this morning. Spirits don't weigh anything, you see."

"How did you know about that?" Lizzie demanded. And then, suddenly, everything became clear.

"So that's why Neil didn't speak to me and …"

"Yes," Jan cut in kindly

"Oh thank God," Lizzie sighed. "I just thought he didn't love me anymore. And that explains why no-one saw me this morning ..."

"Exactly."

Then the truth began to hit.

"But I don't want to be dead," exclaimed Lizzie.

"Oh really?" Jim studied some papers on the desk. "Did you or did you not say to your boyfriend on 12th April at 7.38 a.m., 'I hope there's a bus crash and I'm killed on the way to work'?"

"But everyone hates their job," Lizzie protested.

Jim continued, "Did you not say to Sinead about the break-up of her relationship on January 27th at 9.04 p.m., 'Life's a bitch.'?"

"And then you become one," Lizzie muttered. "Maybe I did."

"Remember one time when you tried to give up smoking and couldn't? And Sinead said to you, 'Don't worry, life's too short.' Remember?"

Lizzie nodded uncomfortably.

"Do you deny that you replied, 'No, it isn't, life's too bloody long'?" Jim paused and looked gravely at her over the top of his glasses. "Need I go on?"

"Well, I didn't mean those things … I was only joking …" she trailed off awkwardly.

A shock of terrible regret and loss swept over Lizzie. If she really was dead, there was so much that she hadn't done. "I never had a child," she said, sadly. "I never went to India, I never even did a bunjee jump."

Jan looked through a list on her desk and said briskly, "Yes, that's absolutely correct."

She ran her finger along the page and continued, "Also, you never read *War and Peace*. Never learnt a foreign language. Never won money on a horse. Never joined the Mile High Club. Never tasted caviar, not that you'd want to, dear, take it from me. Never returned next-door's corkscrew after that party you had last year. Never dyed your hair red and had it cut short — and you have gone on about doing that for most of your thirty-two years, haven't you? Never understood Cubism *and* …" Jan stopped suddenly, "Sorry, am I upsetting you?"

"What do you think?" Lizzie demanded.

"Sorry," Jan said. "I haven't been doing this for long."

"It shows."

"Ah now," Jim said. "She's doing her best."

"But why didn't anyone warn me?" exclaimed Lizzie. "Why didn't anyone tell me that I'd feel like this?"

"But you were warned."

"WHEN!?" Lizzie was horrified. To think that she could have avoided this!

"Didn't you ever hear the saying, Life is not a dress rehearsal?" Jim prompted.

And when Lizzie thought about it, she remembered that someone had said it to her only about a week ago. She'd paid no attention to it. Well, how was she to know that she was going to die!

"And how about, You get no second chances in this life?" reminded Jan.

And yes, Lizzie had to admit that she'd also heard that little saying. A little saying that she had dismissed as annoying nonsense for most of her life.

"Not to mention, You only get one life, so make the most of it?"

"All right, all right! So I got plenty of warnings. I just didn't know that's what they were. I wish I had," she said sadly. "I'd give anything to have another try. I'd really do things differently if I could go back. Just for a week. Or a couple of days. Even a few hours would do. I'd sort things out with Neil. I'd ring my father and tell him that I love him. I've never told him that since I was about five years old."

Suddenly Lizzie was hit by a great idea. "Hey, is this like that film? The one with Jimmy Stewart in it?" she began, in wild excitement. "Where he says he wishes he had never been born. Then an angel makes it happen. But the world is far worse without him. So he gets to go back and he's really glad he's alive?" She stared at them, her face mad with hope.

Jim and Jan shared a sad look.

Jim shook his head. "You wouldn't *believe* the number of people who latch onto that idea."

"*It's a Wonderful Life*, that's what it's called," Lizzie said, still clinging to hope.

Jim shook his head again. "Sorry, Lizzie. I'm afraid that if you're dead, you stay dead. There are no second chances."

"Please," Lizzie begged, her voice tiny.

"It's not up to me," Jim said.

"Ah, go on."

"Honest. It's not up to me. The whole point is you had plenty of time while you were alive. People only come back from the dead in children's fairy tales. Oh yes and the Bible, of course," he added.

Jan gave Jim an admiring look. He was so tough. Would she ever be as good as him? she wondered.

Lizzie sat very still. She was furious at the thought of all her missed chances.

"So what happens now?" she spat. Her voice shook with rage and grief. "Do I go to Hell or what?"

"Oh, I wouldn't have thought you'll be going to Hell." Jan looked into a file on the desk. "You haven't led a bad life. Not entirely blameless either; I don't think anyone will nominate you for the sainthood."

She paused to tinkle at her own wit while Lizzie gazed at her sourly.

"Ah, sorry. Just my little joke," Jan said, humbly. "But you have worked here for a very long time. And you did go out with an estate agent for a while. Both of these will go on your account as a credit under the 'Hell on Earth' scheme."

She laughed again and Lizzie wanted to kill her. "Give me that!" She tried to grab the file.

"I'm sorry, it's none of your business."

"But this is my *life* we're talking about!"

"Not any more, it's not," Jim said. "In fact, strictly speaking, it was never really your life to begin with. It was given to you on loan but could be recalled at any moment, without notice. As you found out to your cost."

"I see," Lizzie said bitterly.

"I was only kidding about Hell," Jan smiled. "There's no such place. By the way, in case you haven't already noticed, there will be some unpleasant side effects as a result of your death."

"Yeah, like being dead!" Lizzie was in no mood.

Jan stared at her with patient and gentle eyes. Then she continued, "You might experience nausea, feelings of doom, fear and loneliness," before adding kindly, "A bit like a bad hangover."

Lizzie sat in sulky silence. Until, out of curiosity, she was forced to speak. "Look, what's going to happen to me?"

"You'll be fine. In a few days you'll see."

"So what am I supposed to do until then?"

"Whatever you like. Watch a bit of telly. Visit yourself in the funeral home. Or you could attend your own funeral. Most people seem to get a kick out of that."

"When is it on?"

"The day after tomorrow. Ten o'clock. Don't be late."

Lizzie realised something. All her life she'd been late for everything. People were forever telling her she'd be late for her own funeral. Well, this was her chance to prove them wrong.

Chapter Nine

Lizzie went home. She could have stayed at work, but why should she? Especially now that they'd stopped paying her. She passed the rest of the day lying on the couch watching good crap on the telly. *Oprah* and *Countdown* and *Home and Away*.

Spending a day like this was the kind of thing she'd longed to do when she was snowed under with work. But now that she had all eternity to do so, it didn't hold the same appeal. She had to admit that it wasn't much fun being dead.

But it wasn't all bad. On the plus side she found she didn't need her bike to get around. She could simply appear anywhere she put her mind to it. She could have gone as far away as Italy or India. She could even have popped up in Brad Pitts's bedroom if she'd really wanted. But she couldn't be bothered. She wanted to stay close to the familiar. Things were difficult enough.

Later that day, as soon as she felt up to it, she visited her mother and father. She watched her mother cry as though her heart was breaking. The guilt was terrible.

"It's too unnatural," her mother wept, "for a parent to bury a child."

Like most people Lizzie hadn't always seen eye-to-eye with her parents. Not that they'd been at each other's throats either. But she realised now she could have spent more time with them. *Should* have spent more time with them. But she had always been so busy. There was always so much to do ...

She was sorry now. Very sorry. With terrible tenderness she watched her mother. She hated the wails that were being pulled from her gut. But when she tried putting her arms around her, her mother shivered as though she was freezing.

Later she went back to her flat and waited for Neil. He'd been running around all day with Sinead, organising the funeral.

When he came home that night, she tried to snuggle up to him in bed. But he shook so badly that she realised that it was better not to touch him.

The thing was, she kept forgetting she was dead. When she saw how upset Neil was by her death, she couldn't stop thinking it was a good thing. That this was exactly what was needed to bring him to his senses. The commitment from him was as good as in the bag. Maybe they'd get married the following spring.

Then she'd think, But hold on a minute. I'm dead. How can we get married if I'm dead?

And then she was angry. She wasn't finished yet. She wasn't ready to let go of being alive. There was so much still to do. She was meant to live until she was at least seventy. And here she was, not even half that, and already out of the game.

The following day, to pass the time, she dropped in to see herself in the funeral home. She couldn't get over her shattered skull. "*Ouch*!" she winced. "Tense, nervous headache? I bet that hurt."

And while she studied herself, she realised something else. She'd been a nice-looking girl. While she'd been alive she'd never been happy with the way she'd looked. The usual list of complaints. Arse too big, boobs too small, hair too frizzy, ears too sticky-outy. But she hadn't known how lucky she was. Whatever about arses and hair and all the rest, at least her skull hadn't been in twenty-seven separate pieces.

After that she went into work. She'd always wanted to be a fly on a wall. Just so she could find out who her friends really were. But it was no good. It was impossible to find out what any of the people she had worked with really thought of her. Because they were too busy saying all the things people say about dead people. "She was a lovely girl." "God takes the good ones young." "At least she lived life to the full." "The place won't be the same without her."

When it became clear that no one was going to do the dirty on her, she hid a couple of highly important files. But her heart wasn't really in it.

Chapter Ten

The morning of the funeral Lizzie popped along to the church to see herself lying in the coffin. Though her make-up was all right, she was very cross to see that she was wearing pink. "How could they?" She was raging. "Everyone knows it doesn't suit me. I look like death."

Her heart lurched when Neil appeared, looking handsome and grim in a black suit. Carefully he placed a huge wreath beside the coffin. Pity he didn't give me those flowers while I was alive, she thought sadly. They're very little use to me now.

At the very last minute, in ran Sinead. Sweet, sparky Sinead. "Sorry I'm late," she gasped.

Lizzie admired Sinead's suit. It was a nice, narrow-cut black one. But even though it was new, already the hem was hanging. Lately, Sinead always looked like she was fraying and unravelling. She needed a break.

Lizzie nearly burst with fondness — and longing. She missed her best pal. She hated not being able to talk to her. It was one of the worst things about being dead — apart from being dead, that was. With a real passion she badly wanted life to work out for Sinead. The way it hadn't for her.

The funeral Mass turned out to be a well-attended affair — long-lost cousins and old school friends and neighbours all showed up. It wasn't unlike Lizzie's 21st birthday party. She really hadn't known that so many people cared about her. She felt the by-now-familiar wash of bitter regret that she'd only found out when it was too late.

Everyone had lovely things to say about Lizzie. The priest just went to town on her. She was, "kind, hard-working, a great story-teller. A good daughter, employee, friend."

Paid her television licence. Always stood her round. As good as invented a cure for cancer.

"Ah stop." Lizzie was hot with pride. "I'm mortified."

Then Neil gave a speech and played a blinder. He spoke about his love for Lizzie. How he wished he'd shown it more while she'd been alive. He had them all in the palm of his hand. Seventy per cent of them were openly weeping. Then, all of a sudden, the mood of enjoyable sorrow was broken. By a horrible, quavery version of 'The Camptown Races'. A mobile-phone moment.

Everyone present turned and glared at a scarlet Sinead.

"Sorry," she whispered. She looked at the caller-display panel, and switched the phone off. "My boss."

Lizzie's aunt leant over and muttered to Michael who worked at the off-licence nearest to Lizzie's flat, "What kind of boss rings a person when they're at their best friend's funeral?"

And Lizzie had to agree. It was crazy carry-on.

When the service ended Lizzie suddenly became aware of certain changes in the way she felt. The nausea and feelings of doom and isolation were definitely getting fainter. When she saw her parents and Sinead and Neil crying, the sorrow wasn't as bad as it had been a couple of days before. Now she could watch their grief with some distance.

And as for her own, as yet unknown, future a calmness had crept in and settled inside her.

After she'd been buried and the mourners had gone their separate ways, Jim and Jan caught up with her.

"How was your funeral?" Jim asked.

"Lovely. You'd want to have seen the crowds!"

"And how do you feel now?"

"Not at all bad, actually."

"Great." .

"There's just one thing …"

There usually is, their faces said.

"I feel …" she tried to find the right word, "…regret about the way I only half-lived my life …"

Jim and Jan were looking at her. Their faces were giving nothing away.

"I wish I'd known," Lizzie pushed on. "I'd have done things differently. I'd have made the very most of my life. And I wondered if there was any chance I could tell this to … some people?"

"What people?" Jim asked. "Neil?"

"Well, I'm not so worried about him. Neil is very good at living life to the full. It's why he didn't want to marry me, that's very clear to me now. No, the person I was really thinking of was Sinead."

Jim and Jan raised their eyebrows at each other. "Why not?"

"So what should I do? I don't want to scare her."

"Grand. Well, appearing in a dream is a popular way."

"Can I pop by and visit my parents too?"

"Ah, sure, you might as well."

"And Neil?"

"Go on then. While you're at it."

Chapter Eleven

First Lizzie visited her parents and had a lovely talk with both of them at the same time. She told them to make the most of the many years they had left. Then she told them that she was fine and that she loved them both. "Even me?" her dad pressed. "Even though I never spoke to you when you used to ring up."

"Of course."

"That's nice," he murmured.

"Shergar," she added.

"Ah stop," he said.

"I'm only messing. Bye Mum, bye Dad."

In the morning they both remembered their dream in exactly the same way. Right down to the smallest detail.

"She called you Shergar," Mrs Whelan said.

"She did," Mr Whelan agreed.

They both agreed that she had actually visited them. It gave them some comfort, over the days and weeks and months ahead, when the grief got too much to bear.

Next on Lizzie's list was Neil.

"I should have loved you better," he said. "I didn't mean to be unkind. You know …"

"… that was the last thing on your mind. Have some respect for the dead," Lizzie chided with good humour. "Spare me the song lyrics."

"Sorry. I did love you, I just wasn't very good at showing it."

"Well, you'll know better the next time."

"Will there be a next time?"

"Oh yes."

"With you?"

"Cripes no. Someone else."

"And you don't mind?"

"Not in the slightest."

"Janey, there is a God."

Last call was to Sinead.

"How's it going," Sinead said sleepily. "But you're meant to be dead."

"Oh, I am," Lizzie agreed. "I just wanted to have a quick word. I'd like you to do something for me."

"What's that?"

"Don't wait until you're dead to want to live your life. Just do it. Go to Italy or Greece or Paris or *somewhere*. You're always saying you're going to."

"Only when I'm drunk," Sinead mumbled. "And what would I live on?"

"Teach English. Work in a bar — it doesn't matter. Making a living isn't the important thing. Living is."

"Easy for you to say. You're dead."

"That's right, and I should know."

"I'm very busy right now," Sinead said. "But I've got plans. For when the time is right."

"Life is what happens while we're busy making plans," Lizzie said smugly.

"You've changed," Sinead complained. "You usen't to be such a know-all."

"That's being dead for you," Lizzie said cheerfully.

"Do you mind?" Sinead mumbled. "Being dead?"

Lizzie thought about it. The changes that had happened after the funeral had continued. The white, numb feelings of peace had grown stronger. Even the urgent need to talk to Sinead had calmed down a lot.

"I'm fine," she promised Sinead. "Now swear to me that you'll tell Ginger Moran to stick his job. Go on, life isn't a dress rehearsal."

"I'll think about it. Call again," Sinead invited sleepily.

"No. This is a once-in-a-lifetime-opportunity."

"OK," Sinead said slackly and fell back to sleep.

Her last visit completed, Lizzie was feeling wonderful. Far better than any dead person had a right to feel, she thought. So what happens next?

She looked down at her body, and was in no way surprised to see that it was gone. There was just silvery air where once she had been. The fantastic feeling of well-being built and swelled. She was calm, she was safe, she was joyous. And there was no alarm when she felt her spirit melting. Something rushed though her, then the last of Lizzie was speeding away like a genie spinning back into the bottle. Yet she sparkled through everything in a tingle of glitter. Reforming and reconnecting. Into every drop of rain, every blade of grass, every word spoken.

Blissful, happy, ever-present nothingness. White-out.

Sinead woke up to a moment's blessed blankness, then she remembered that Lizzie was dead. But it didn't crash in on top of her like a belt from a hammer, the way it had done the last two mornings. She was surprised by how calm she felt.

A vague memory of a dream floated about in her head. She couldn't manage to hold onto it. But it was something nice, something good ... And a strange peace worked its way through her.

Until she began to get ready for work, that is. The memory of Ginger ringing her at Lizzie's funeral made her furious.

"That bloody job," she raged. "That bloody Ginger. I'm going to leave. One day I'll just hand in my notice and then he'll be sorry. I really will. One day soon."

Her head filled with Italian images. Mornings lit by yellow sunshine. Purple flowers against a wall so blindingly white it hurt to look at it. Lying in hot, gritty sand with some unknown, perfect man.

"One day," she promised herself grimly, as she tried to find something to wear to work.

She rooted around in her linen basket, looking for her cleanest dirty shirt. Suddenly, a perky thought lit up out of nowhere. The time is now. The time is always now.

Actually, I won't hand in my notice some day, she thought, her heart soaring. I'll do it today.

ALSO IN THIS SERIES:

JOE'S WEDDING by Gareth O'Callaghan

It is the morning of Joe's wedding. He opens his eyes to find himself on a park bench beside the sea, dressed in torn tights and a cape. And that's not his only chilly awakening. For Joe is in Holyhead, but his wedding is in Dublin. And he doesn't even remember how he got there.

As Joe tries to put the pieces back together, an old man joins him on the bench. Marty is a local, no stranger to these parts. So how does he know so much about this gruff young man? And why is he so interested in talking to a stranger in a Superman suit, who clearly has no time for chit-chat? That's hardly going to help Joe solve his major dilemma: Does he really want to get married? And it's certainly not going to help get him to the church on time if he does.

Or will it …?

THE COMEDIAN by Joseph O'Connor

It is 1975 in a small town near Dublin. The Bay City Rollers are topping the charts. Starsky and Hutch rule the television screen. In Northern Ireland, bombs are going off. And here, in this little town on the sea, a young boy's life is about to be changed forever.

By day his father is a delivery man for the local bakery. He dreams of being a comedian by night — a famous performer, a hero, a star. But the future that is lying in wait for this family, in a story of childhood both funny and sad, will turn their whole world upside down.

SECOND CHANCE by Patricia Scanlan

Tony O'Neill is not having a good day. He is unemployed and broke, with a wife and child to support. Even worse, he's living with his snooty mother-in-law. They don't get on.

Bridie Feeny is very annoyed. She's just had a row with her son-in-law and her daughter, Jean. Bitter words have been spoken. But she is *not* going to apologise.
Dave Cummins needs a fix … badly. It's the worst day of his life. He knows he's going to do something he swore he'd never do.

Sarah Collins is looking forward to a day in town. It's been planned for ages … then the unthinkable happens!

It's a day none of them will ever forget. But for Tony and Jean it's the day they get a second chance.

PIPE DREAMS by Anne Schulman

Meany Freeney is a bachelor farmer with simple needs and a healthy bank balance. His take on life could be summed up by his drinking habits — why buy a pint of Guinness when a half-pint, sipped slowly, gives twice the value?

Trouble brews when an old flame arrives back in town. Her sparkle lights up his lonely world, but if he and the free-spending Julie are ever to marry, Meany must loosen his iron grip on the purse strings.

Soon there is talk of fancy central heating, hot running water, and even a gas cooker! But Meany has some cost-saving plans up his sleeve that should keep everyone happy. Or so he thinks …

OLD MONEY, NEW MONEY by Peter Sheridan

The city is Dublin, the year is 1972.

Redser and Pancho are two teenagers from the North Wall. Redser is top of the class, especially good at maths. Pancho's knack is for finding money, not adding or subtracting it. Redser's parents run the local credit union. Pancho's dad runs riot in the city pubs on pay day. The boys' worlds could not be further apart. Yet the pair are the best of friends.

One day, on his regular paper round, Redser stumbles upon the aftermath of a crime. Two elderly sisters, 'the East Wall witches', have been burgled. But the robbers haven't taken all the money.

Redser and Pancho are about to face their biggest dilemma ever ...

SERIES I

SAD SONG by Vincent Banville

John Blaine is a private detective, who walks Dublin's mean streets. He is tough and smart, but unlucky in love — his wife has just left him. Hired to bring home a straying daughter, he takes the girl's side against her rich father, and suffers for it.

Gripping, funny and stripped to the bone, *Sad Song* is a short novel that packs a punch like a fist in a velvet glove ...

IN HIGH GERMANY by Dermot Bolger

Eoin tells his son the story of Euro '88.

The excitement is high for football fanatics like Eoin, Shane and Mick, who all work abroad. Now they are in Germany supporting the Irish team, witnessing the highs and the lows.

For these emigrant friends, home is no longer where the heart is. Home is where the Irish team plays, and there will be many adventures on and off the pitch before the final whistle blows.

Also included is *A Poet's Notebook*: a selection of short poems about ordinary life by the author, with his notes on how and why they were written.

NOT JUST FOR CHRISTMAS by Roddy Doyle

Danny Murphy is going to meet his brother, Jimmy. They haven't seen each other in over twenty years. On the way to the meeting, Danny remembers the good times and the bad times, the fun and the fights — and the one big row that drove them apart. Will they fight again or will they become the friends they used to be?

Danny doesn't know.

MAGGIE'S STORY by Sheila O'Flanagan

Maggie is forty-three years old and looking for romance. She loves her husband, Dan, but his idea of romance is a couple of drinks at the local and an early night at home.

Her children think she's too old to care. And she's beginning to wonder if life has passed her by. But a chance meeting changes all that, and now Maggie faces tough decisions. Can she put the spark back into her marriage, or would she be better off calling it a day? And who is more important? Her husband? Her children?

Or herself?

JESUS AND BILLY ARE OFF TO BARCELONA
by Deirdre Purcell

Billy is an average-looking sixteen-year-old who lives in an ordinary Dublin estate on the northside of the city. Jesus, on the other hand, is a beautiful boy with Continental manners, from the poshest part of Barcelona. He travels from Spain to live with Billy's family for three weeks one summer. The plan is that at the end of the holiday, Billy will go back with Jesus on a return visit. However, no one should make plans ...

RIPPLES by Patricia Scanlan

The McHughs' marriage is on the rocks.

Daughter Ciara worries that her mother and father are going to divorce. Lillian, Ciara's Gran, is worried too. She has a nice life now, since her bullying husband died. This could all change. Meanwhile, Brenda Johnston is very happy. She has a lot to gain if the McHughs divorce. Or has she?

And Mike and Kathy Stuart, the McHughs' best friends, are beginning to wonder if the friendship can survive.

Then, one awful night, everything changes ...

See overleaf for ordering details

ORDER FORM

___ *No Dress Rehearsal* **by Marian Keyes**
    ISBN: 1 902602 32 3, £4.99

___ *Joe's Wedding* **by Gareth O'Callaghan**
    ISBN: 1 902602 35 8, £4.99

___ *The Comedian* **by Joseph O'Connor**
    ISBN: 1 902602 37 4 , £4.99

___ *Second Chance* **by Patricia Scanlan**
    ISBN: 1 902602 33 1, £4.99

___ *Pipe Dreams* **by Anne Schulman**
    ISBN: 1 902602 34 X, £4.99

___ *Old Money, New Money* **by Peter Sheridan**
    ISBN: 1 902602 36 6, £4.99

___ *Sad Song* **by Vincent Banville**
    ISBN: 1 902602 18 8, £4.99

___ *In High Germany* **by Dermot Bolger**
    ISBN: 1 902602 14 5, £4.99

___ *Not Just for Christmas* **by Roddy Doyle**
    ISBN: 1 902602 15 3, £4.99

___ *Maggie's Story* **by Sheila O'Flanagan**
    ISBN: 1 902602 17 X, £4.99

___ *Jesus and Billy Are Off to Barcelona* **by Deirdre Purcell**
    ISBN: 1 902602 13 1, £4.99

___ *Ripples* **by Patricia Scanlan**
    ISBN: 1 902602 13 7, £4.99

TRADE ORDERS TO:
CMD, 55A Spruce Avenue,
Stillorgan Industrial Park, Blackrock, Co Dublin, Ireland.
Tel. (+353 1) 294 2560
Fax. (+353 1) 294 2564

EDUCATIONAL AND PERSONAL ORDERS TO:
New Island Books, 2 Brookside, Dundrum Road,
Dundrum, Dublin 14, Ireland.
Tel: (+353 1) 298 9937/298 3411
Fax: (+353 1) 298 2783
E-Mail: nibsales@brookside.iol.ie
Please include a cheque or postal order for the amount
payable to New Island Books,
plus £2 for post and packaging.